ANTELOPE,
BISON,
COUGAR

ANTELOPE, BISON, COUGAR

Steven P. Medley
Illustrated by Daniel San Souci

A NATIONAL PARK WILDLIFE ALPHABET BOOK

YOSEMITE ASSOCIATION
Yosemite National Park, California

For Hermie, with appreciation for her example, encouragement, love, and support over the years.—S.P.M.

For my family, who went way beyond the call of duty for support and enthusiasm while I worked on this book.
Special thanks to Roland Smith and Greg Treat for their expertise on wildlife.—D.S.S.

Yosemite Association
P.O. Box 230
El Portal, CA 95318

The Yosemite Association initiates and supports interpretive, educational, research, scientific, and
environmental programs in Yosemite National Park, in cooperation with the National Park Service.
Authorized by Congress, the Association provides services and direct financial support in order to
promote park stewardship and enrich the visitor experience.

To learn more about our activities and other publications, or for information about membership,
please write to the address above or call (209) 379-2646. Our web site address is: www.yosemite.org

Design by Kathy Warinner, Aufuldish & Warinner, San Anselmo, California.

All illustrations by Daniel San Souci. The paintings were made with Winsor & Newton watercolors
(highlighted in some cases with Berol Prismacolor pencils) on 300 lb. De Arches paper. The drawings
were made using 3B Derwent pencils on 100 lb. Strathmore Bristol paper.

Printed in Singapore.

ABOUT THIS BOOK

This alphabet book was created to introduce young people to the wealth of mammals, birds, and other creatures that live in various sites throughout the U.S. national park system. Each species is portrayed in a different park locale to demonstrate the variety of natural areas that exists within that system.

The youngest reader can enjoy the book by associating the letters of the alphabet with different animals and by studying the true-to-life drawings and paintings that illustrate the work. Older children can learn more and in greater depth from the information provided about the various wild creatures and about the national park areas included in the volume.

At the rear of the book is a map illustrating the locations of the parks, contact information for the National Park Service and the sites in the park system included in this book, and a listing of national organizations that work to support wildlife and national parks generally.

We hope this publication will stimulate in readers of all ages an interest in, a love for, and a desire to protect America's wild animals and the national park areas where they make their homes.

Steven P. Medley and Daniel San Souci

A IS FOR ANTELOPE

The pronghorn antelope is the fastest animal in North America. Throughout the world, only the African cheetah runs faster. Their speed (up to 60 miles per hour) allows these antelopes to escape animals hunting them, and their excellent eyesight gives them the ability to see predators that are three or more miles away.

Jenny Lake, located at the western base of the Teton Range, was created by the hollowing action of the glaciers.

GRAND TETON NATIONAL PARK showcases the beauty of Wyoming's Teton mountain range that rises steeply above the Snake River and the valley called Jackson Hole. The park is important because it protects the Tetons and several critical wildlife habitats, including pine forests, sagebrush plains, and lakes. It is home to a remarkable variety of birds (trumpeter swans and sandhill cranes), mammals (elk, grizzly bear, and moose), wildflowers, and other living things.

This antelope earned its name from its pronged horns growing as long as 18 inches. Made up of a bony core covered by a black outer sheath, the horns are shed every year.

GRAND TETON NATIONAL PARK

B IS FOR BISON

The bison, also called the buffalo, is the largest mammal on the North American continent. A full-grown male bison can weigh up to 2,000 pounds (a ton), and be over six feet tall at the shoulder. Despite their size, bison are very good swimmers, and float with their head, hump, and tail projecting above the water.

These strange, mushroom-like formations, created by the erosion of fire-hardened rocks, are called "cannonball concretions."

THEODORE ROOSEVELT NATIONAL PARK was established as a memorial to President Theodore Roosevelt for his lasting contributions to the protection of America's natural and cultural treasures. The park is important because it protects over 700,000 acres in the Little Missouri Badlands of North Dakota, an area with colorful banded formations. Park wildlife includes bison (reintroduced in 1956), elk, prairie dogs, and over 180 species of birds.

The head of the bison is huge and covered with a thick mat of wiry hair. The short, black, pointed horns are never shed.

THEODORE ROOSEVELT NATIONAL PARK

C IS FOR COUGAR

The largest member of the cat family in North America, the cougar is also known as the mountain lion, the panther, and the puma. Weighing from 80 to 180 pounds, cougars are easily identified by their long, heavy tails that are tipped with black. Cougars are not very active during the day (except in undisturbed areas) and so are rarely seen.

This natural arch is one of many fantastic park formations. Upright columns and pinnacles are called "hoodoos."

BRYCE CANYON NATIONAL PARK is located on a plateau in southern Utah. The park is important because it protects an area where erosion has shaped colorful limestones, sandstones, and mudstones into thousands of forms including spires, fins, and pinnacles. From the rim of the plateau, panoramic views of three states spread beyond the park's boundaries. Because it has no major sources of artificial light at night, Bryce Canyon offers great stargazing.

The eyesight of the cougar is extraordinary, with a wide field of view. Because the jaw is not long and comes equipped with large muscles, this cat has a powerful bite.

BRYCE CANYON NATIONAL PARK

D IS FOR DEER

The mule deer is very common in national parks and undeveloped areas from California through the Rocky Mountains. Males grow antlers that are covered in velvet each summer. Mule deer eat acorns, grass, and twigs from such plants as deerbrush, berry bushes, and willows. When descending a hill, these deer make bounds up to 25 feet long.

Dome-shaped Moro Rock offers a spectacular view of Sequoia National Park. Visitors can climb a steep series of steps with railings to its 6,725-foot top.

SEQUOIA NATIONAL PARK is located in the southern Sierra Nevada of California. The park is important because it protects large numbers of beautiful giant sequoia trees, many of them several thousand years old, and the extensive wilderness around them. The largest trees on Earth, the huge sequoias can be 300 feet tall, 100 feet around, and weigh as much as 1,000 tons. The park also is home to the highest peak in the continental United States, Mt. Whitney.

Baby deer, called fawns, are born in early summer with spots that help them hide from other animals. The spots disappear in the autumn when the fawns grow a winter coat.

SEQUOIA NATIONAL PARK

E IS FOR E L K

The Roosevelt elk lives in the rain forests of the Pacific Coast, from Vancouver Island down to northern California. These animals are very large (up to 900 pounds) and have dark-colored manes of hair. Favorite foods are huckleberry, blackberry, grasses, weeds, and vines. Feeding is done just after daylight and again in the evening.

Numerous rock formations, natural arches, and tiny islands called "sea stacks" are scattered along the Olympic coastline.

OLYMPIC NATIONAL PARK is located in northwest Washington overlooking the rugged Pacific Coast. The park is important because it protects the largest remaining undisturbed old-growth and temperate rain forests in the Pacific Northwest. Nearly 95% of the park is set aside as wilderness, and it includes sixty miles of wild and undeveloped coastline. Animals and plants unique to the park include Olympic torrent salamanders, tiger beetles, Flett's violets, and Olympic marmots.

The antlers of the male elk are huge, heavy, and spreading. They grow in the late summer and early fall.

OLYMPIC NATIONAL PARK

F IS FOR FALCON

The peregrine falcon is one of the world's fastest flying birds, reaching speeds of up to 200 miles per hour. Until recently, the peregrine was considered an endangered species in the United States, but with the drop in use of the harmful pesticide DDT, this beautiful bird has made a dramatic recovery. Peregrines nest on Yosemite Valley's steep granite walls.

Yosemite Falls in Yosemite Valley is one of the highest waterfalls in the world, dropping 2,425 feet in three sections.

YOSEMITE NATIONAL PARK is located in the Sierra Nevada mountains of California. The park is important because it preserves a large area of high country wilderness, three groves of giant sequoia trees, and the remarkable Yosemite Valley, where glaciers created impressive waterfalls, cliffs, and unusual rock formations. Yosemite provides a home for over 400 species of animals and almost 1,500 different plants. It offers excellent hiking, climbing, and backpacking.

The peregrine feeds mainly on other birds such as ducks, pigeons, and gulls. These powerful falcons capture their prey in mid-air, diving down from high above and seizing them in their sharp talons.

YOSEMITE NATIONAL PARK

G IS FOR GRIZZLY

The grizzly bear once roamed throughout the lower 48 United States, but now lives only in Montana, Wyoming, Washington, and Idaho. Grizzlies are still fairly common in Alaska and Canada, however. While the huge bears may appear slow and lumbering, they can climb trees, swim through fast currents, and run up to 35 miles per hour for short distances.

Chief Mountain, 9,080 feet high, is a prominent landmark on the route to Waterton Lakes, and an important spiritual site for the Blackfeet and other native people.

GLACIER NATIONAL PARK, located in upper Montana, shares its northern border with Waterton Lakes National Park in Alberta, Canada. The two parks make up Waterton-Glacier International Peace Park, which is dedicated to cooperative stewardship of shared resources by two countries. Glacier is important because it protects over a million acres with spectacular scenery and a wide variety of plants and animals in one of the largest undisturbed ecosystems in North America.

Mother grizzlies give birth to one or more cubs in late January or early February. The cubs are cared for by their mothers for 2 to 3 years before they strike out on their own.

GLACIER NATIONAL PARK

H IS FOR HAWK

The red-tailed hawk has broad wings and a wide, rounded tail that is reddish-brown on its upper surface. Common throughout the United States, red-tails are regularly seen soaring in wide circles or perching on treetops and poles. They drop from the air in a steep dive to capture ground squirrels, mice, gophers, snakes, and lizards to eat.

Angels Landing, standing 1,435 feet above the floor of Zion Canyon, is reached by a strenuous, narrow trail with zigzagging switchbacks and long dropoffs.

ZION NATIONAL PARK is located in southwest Utah, on the edge of the Colorado Plateau. The park is important because it protects a 229-square-mile landscape of brilliantly-colored rock canyons and sandstone cliffs (much of it wilderness), along with the living things that inhabit it. Zion is home to the richest diversity of plants in Utah – over 800 native species – and contains Kolob Arch, the world's largest with a span that measures 310 feet.

The eyesight of the red-tailed hawk is very good, allowing it to notice movement on the ground from high above. The hawk's beak is hooked to help with eating prey.

ZION NATIONAL PARK

I IS FOR IBIS

The white ibis is the most common wading bird found in the Everglades. Most of the long-legged birds that wade into the water catch fish to eat, but the ibis dines primarily on crayfish. It uses its long, slender, curved beak to probe the mud in search of such food. Ibises are often seen in large flocks flying in a long line or in a V-shaped formation.

Florida Bay and the rest of the Florida coastline within the park are lined with shallow-water basins, grassy banks, and mangrove islands.

EVERGLADES NATIONAL PARK is located in southern Florida and includes many miles of coastline along with large areas of sawgrass, freshwater marsh, open Everglades prairie, and mangrove forest. The park is important because it protects the largest remaining subtropical wilderness in the United States. Everglades wildlife includes rare and endangered species, such as the American crocodile, Florida panther, and West Indian manatee.

The nest of the white ibis is a loosely-built platform of sticks usually located in trees from 3 to 15 feet above the water. Normally, several nests are grouped together.

EVERGLADES NATIONAL PARK

J IS FOR JAVELINA

The javelina (pronounced *have-uh-leen-a*) is a native pig-like animal also known as the collared peccary. Javelinas, in groups of 2 to 25, usually are active mornings and late afternoons looking for food. They will eat just about anything, including cactus, nuts, berries, grubs, and bird eggs. A typical javelina stands 2 feet high, is 3 feet long, and weighs 40 to 50 pounds.

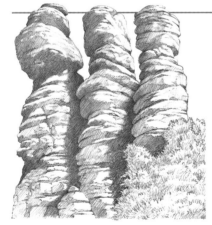

Chiricahua's 17 miles of maintained trails lead through a spectacular landscape offering inspiring views of balanced rocks, towers, and minarets.

CHIRICAHUA NATIONAL MONUMENT is located in the Chiricahua Mountains of southern Arizona near the New Mexico boundary. The monument is important because it protects a collection of pinnacles, spires, and balanced rocks created by erosion of hardened volcanic ash and debris. Because the mountains form an island rising above the arid Chihuahuan and Sonoran deserts, the monument is a refuge for a wide and distinctive variety of plants and animals.

The javelina has a long snout that is flat, free of hair, and round on the end. The snout is pushed around in the soil and under plants and leaves in search of food.

CHIRICAHUA NATIONAL MONUMENT

K IS FOR KINGFISHER

The belted kingfisher can be found in many national parks throughout the country. A bird of wetlands, streams, and open water, the kingfisher perches or hovers, then dives headfirst into water in pursuit of fish. It makes an odd rattling sound as it flies, and has a large, crested head and very short legs. The kingfisher nests in a deep burrow dug in a river bank.

The bays, harbors, and shorelines of Acadia feature striking rock formations, cliffs, and ledges, sometimes protected from the sea and sometimes jutting into it.

ACADIA NATIONAL PARK is located on the northeast coast of Maine and includes sections of the mainland and islands off the shore. The park is important because it protects the undeveloped rockbound coast, the rugged beauty of the seashore, and the nearby mountains and islands. Forty-five miles of rustic carriage roads weave around the mountains and through the valleys of the park, and they are used for hiking, bicycling, and cross-country skiing.

Once the kingfisher has caught a fish in its powerful beak, it flies to a perch, strikes the fish against a tree limb, tosses it into the air, then swallows it headfirst.

ACADIA NATIONAL PARK

L IS FOR LIZARD

The collared lizard has a broad head, a large mouth, and a long, flattened tail. Its rear legs are much larger and stronger than the front legs. These muscular limbs allow the lizard to leap long distances. When frightened, it will rise up and run on its two back legs only. This desert reptile will eat insects, other lizards, and berries, leaves, and flowers on occasion.

There are few paved roads at Canyonlands, and visitors can best access the park by way of its trails, rivers, and 4-wheel drive roads. Their reward is unique sandstone scenery, such as this butte with "hoodoo" formations.

CANYONLANDS NATIONAL PARK is located in southeast Utah. The park is important because it preserves an immense wilderness of rock at the heart of the Colorado Plateau. Water and gravity were the forces that shaped the land, cutting flat layers of sedimentary rock into hundreds of colorful canyons, mesas, buttes, fins, arches, and spires. The centerpieces of the park are two great canyons – those carved by the Green and Colorado Rivers.

This lizard gets its name from the two dark bands or collars that circle its throat. It prefers open areas where plants are sparse and flat rocks for basking in the hot sun are available.

CANYONLANDS NATIONAL PARK

M IS FOR MOOSE

The moose is roughly the size of a horse, with dark brown hair and humped shoulders. A good swimmer, the moose can move through the water at a rate of 6 miles per hour – faster than two men can paddle a canoe. This hooved mammal eats water lilies and willows in the summer, and bark, twigs, and buds from a variety of plants in the winter.

The climb of the Moose's Tooth is one of Denali's many challenging mountaineering routes. The unusually-shaped peak rises high above the Buckskin Glacier.

DENALI NATIONAL PARK is located in the center of Alaska. The park is important because it protects North America's highest mountain, 20,320-foot Mount McKinley, and over 6 million acres in the Alaska Range studded with spectacular peaks and large glaciers. Denali encompasses a complete sub-arctic ecosystem with large mammals, such as grizzly bears, wolves, Dall sheep, and moose. Denali is used by wildlife watchers, mountaineers, and backpackers.

Its huge, flat antlers distinguish the male moose. They start growing in March and are at their largest in August, when their velvet coverings fall off.

DENALI NATIONAL PARK

N IS FOR NĒNĒ

The nēnē (pronounced *nay-nay*) is a native Hawaiian goose and the state bird. Because it lives far from fresh water on the hardened lava flows of volcanoes, it has lost some of the webbing between its toes that most geese use for swimming. Nēnē nest on the lava in feather-lined hollows hidden under shrubs. The nēnē eats only plants, including grass, leaves, and berries.

HAWAI'I VOLCANOES NATIONAL PARK is located on the island of Hawai'i. The park is important because it preserves active volcanoes Kīlauea and Mauna Loa and 217,000 acres around them. Kīlauea, one of the world's most active volcanoes, still pours hot lava into the Pacific Ocean in a spectacular display. The park is a refuge for the island's native plants and animals, and a link to its human past and the unique Hawaiian culture.

The only remaining Hawaiian goose, the nēnē was saved from extinction by a captive breeding program begun in the 1940s. Today there are about 900 nēnē living in the wild, 200 of them in Hawai'i Volcanoes.

When hot lava from Kīlauea enters the ocean, a steam cloud of hydrochloric acid is produced as the lava boils the sea water.

HAWAI'I VOLCANOES NATIONAL PARK

O IS FOR OWL

The elf owl is the smallest owl in the world – about the size of a sparrow and a little larger than a chickadee. It nests in holes that woodpeckers have made in saguaro cactus and a variety of trees. Despite its size, the elf owl has a remarkably loud voice. It makes whistling noises, along with "chucklings" and "yips," so it sounds like a puppy dog.

The saguaro cactus is renowned for the variety of odd, sometimes human shapes it assumes.

SAGUARO NATIONAL PARK is located near Tucson, Arizona, in the Sonoran Desert. The park is important because it protects the giant saguaro cacti (sometimes reaching a height of 50 feet) that cover the valley floor and rise into the Rincon and West Tucson Mountains. It also preserves many other members of the Sonoran Desert community – additional cacti, desert trees and shrubs, and animals. The park is divided into two sections on either side of Tucson.

The elf owl has a round head with yellow eyes and white "eyebrows." Its food is primarily insects, including beetles, moths, grasshoppers, crickets, and scorpions.

SAGUARO NATIONAL PARK

P IS FOR PORCUPINE

The porcupine is about the size of a small dog, with a large body and short legs. It is the only mammal in North America with long, sharp-pointed quills over most of its body. Because its enemies are afraid of these painful quills, they rarely bother this sluggish creature. Though clumsy and slow, the porcupine is more at home in trees than on the ground.

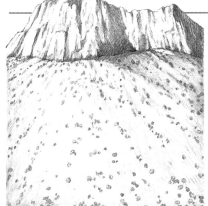

The rim of Crater Lake is 21.5 miles around and rises steeply above its shore. All along the rim are unusual volcanic formations like this lava plug.

CRATER LAKE NATIONAL PARK is located in south central Oregon in the Cascade Mountains. The park is important because it protects the deepest lake in the United States (1,958 feet) and the seventh deepest in the world, along with a 265-square-mile wilderness area of mountains and forests around it. The five-mile-wide lake in the top of an old volcano is remarkably clear primarily because there are no rivers or streams emptying into it.

There are 30,000 spear-like quills on a porcupine, primarily on its back and tail. Though it cannot "shoot" the quills, by swinging its tail the porcupine can drive them deeply into the body of an enemy.

CRATER LAKE NATIONAL PARK

Q IS FOR QUAIL

The California quail is small and plump with a black feather that curves forward from the crown of its head. These birds scratch the soil like chickens in their search for food. Quail form and travel in groups called coveys, and when startled, each bird will fly off in a different direction with a loud whirring of wings.

The imposing granite feature called the Grand Sentinel, here seen from Zumwalt Meadow, stands 8,504 feet high on the south wall of Kings Canyon.

KINGS CANYON NATIONAL PARK is located in the southern Sierra Nevada of California. The park is important because it protects the South and Middle Forks of the splendid Kings River, large wilderness areas, and several awe-inspiring sequoia groves. The main Kings Canyon is a deep, glaciated canyon with exceptional scenery comparable to that of Yosemite Valley. Much of the park is rugged backcountry reached only by trails.

The feather plume of the California quail forms a curve, distinguishing the species from its relative, the mountain quail. The mountain quail sports a long, straight head plume. California and mountain quail are sometimes seen together in the foothills in winter.

KINGS CANYON NATIONAL PARK

R IS FOR RATTLESNAKE

The western rattlesnake, found in most western parks, has many subspecies, including the Hopi rattlesnake found in Petrified Forest National Park. The rattles are small buttons at the end of the tail made of the same substance in human fingernails. A threatened rattlesnake will sound a warning by shaking these buttons, which make a buzzing sound, not a rattle.

The Petrified Forest is decorated with hundreds of unusual formations like this upright petrified trunk.

PETRIFIED FOREST NATIONAL PARK is located in northeastern Arizona. The park is important because it protects one of the world's largest and most colorful concentrations of petrified wood. The petrified logs were created when trees fell into rivers and were carried into the lowlands. The logs were buried by mud, which slowed their decay. When groundwater dissolved silica from volcanic ash and carried it through the logs, it was crystallized as the mineral quartz.

The fangs of the rattlesnake are sharp, hollow, and pointed. They are connected by a hinge to the roof of the snake's mouth, which opens widely so that poison can be injected into prey.

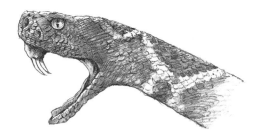

PETRIFIED FOREST NATIONAL PARK

S IS FOR SHEEP

The bighorn sheep is at home in the rocks and cliffs. Its hooves are soft and spongy in the center and hard at the edges, allowing the sheep to maintain excellent traction even when leaping from rock to rock. Moving in groups numbering from 5 to 15, the sheep spend most of the year in the high mountains, then drop down to lower meadows each winter.

This curious formation is known as Mushroom Rock. Located above the Rock Cut area near the Trail Ridge Road, it was created by the action of time and weathering.

ROCKY MOUNTAIN NATIONAL PARK is located in north central Colorado. The park is important because it protects a wilderness area that contains more than 110 peaks that rise above 10,000 feet, more than 100 square miles of alpine tundra, about 150 lakes, and 450 miles of rivers and streams. Rain and melted snow east of the ridge that divides the park flow to the Gulf of Mexico and the Atlantic Ocean, while runoff to its west flows to the Pacific Ocean.

This sheep gets its name from its huge, coiled horns that spiral back, then out, then forward in an almost complete circle. In the fall, male sheep (called rams) butt their horns together as part of their mating ceremony.

ROCKY MOUNTAIN NATIONAL PARK

T IS FOR TARANTULA

The tarantula is a very large spider, sometimes as big as 6 inches across. These lightweight, usually dark-colored creatures are covered with hair. Despite their appearance, tarantulas are very gentle and will not bite unless they feel threatened. Their venom is much weaker than a bee's and not dangerous to humans. Female tarantulas can live to be 30 years old.

Zabriskie Point was created when erosion molded layers of yellow and red clay and mudstones into this striped landscape.

DEATH VALLEY NATIONAL PARK, one of our country's largest, is located in the deserts of southeastern California and southern Nevada. It is important because it protects more than 3.3 million acres of spectacular desert wilderness and unique scenery, a wealth of unusual and rare desert wildlife, and numerous historical sites, many of them related to mining. A spot in the park near Badwater, at 282 feet below sea level, is the lowest point in the western hemisphere.

The hair on the underside of the tarantula is barbed and can cause itching to humans and other animals. When bothered, the spider will use its legs to brush the irritating hairs into the face of its enemies.

DEATH VALLEY NATIONAL PARK

U IS FOR URSUS

Scientists have special names for animals, birds, and plants. The scientific name for the black bear is *Ursus americanus*. The bear's common name is a bit confusing because its color can vary from brown to cinnamon to blond to black. In January or February, female black bears normally give birth to two babies called cubs weighing about half a pound each.

The Chimney Tops got their name because the two rock formations, created by erosion, look like chimneys from a distance. The taller chimney is 4,755 feet high.

GREAT SMOKY MOUNTAINS NATIONAL PARK is located straddling the states of North Carolina and Tennessee. The park is important because it protects 800 square miles of mountain wilderness, 95 percent of which is forested. It features a diversity of plant and animal life, remnants of the Southern Appalachian mountain culture, and fine backpacking and hiking opportunities. Great Smokies is one of the largest areas of land preserved in the eastern United States.

Both adult and young black bears are very good climbers, and cubs oftentimes are sent up trees to avoid disturbances or trouble.

GREAT SMOKY MOUNTAINS NATIONAL PARK

V IS FOR VULTURE

The turkey vulture is often seen soaring high in the sky, its wings forming the shape of a broad, flattened V. It tilts quickly from side to side as it looks for food on the ground, making use of its excellent eyesight. These large birds mainly eat dead animals, and when one vulture finds something to feast on, it is joined by others.

Grand Canyon's inner canyon can only be reached on foot or muleback, though many whitewater rafters make the challenging trip on the river each year.

GRAND CANYON NATIONAL PARK is located in northern Arizona. The park is important because it protects nearly 280 miles of the Colorado River canyon that averages ten miles across and a mile deep. A spectacular example of erosion, the Grand Canyon offers unmatched views of colorful sandstone formations and other geological wonders. Visitors to the park can enjoy hiking, river rafting, camping, sightseeing, and many other activities.

The head of the turkey vulture has no feathers (so that it won't get dirty while eating), and its beak is sharp, heavy, and hooked. The bird's keen eyesight and sense of smell help it find food.

GRAND CANYON NATIONAL PARK

W IS FOR WOLF

Gray wolves once roamed across most of North America. In the 1920s, most wolves in the United States had been killed because people thought wolves threatened them and their livestock. Now protected as an endangered species, the gray wolf was returned to Yellowstone in 1995 and 1996. Healthy packs of wolves once again make the park their home.

The most famous of Yellowstone's 250 active geysers is Old Faithful. It now usually erupts about every 80 minutes.

YELLOWSTONE NATIONAL PARK, located in northwestern Wyoming and extending into Montana and Idaho, is one of the most famous natural preserves on Earth. Established in 1872, Yellowstone was the first national park in the world. The park is important because it protects an immense area of wilderness with impressive geologic, geothermal, and natural features, including steaming geysers, colorful canyons, roaring waterfalls, and abundant wildlife.

Wolves are known for their howls, the haunting calls by which they communicate. Each wolf has a unique howl, recognized by the other wolves.

YELLOWSTONE NATIONAL PARK

X IS FOR BLACKBIRD

The scientific name for the yellow-headed blackbird is *Xanthocephalus xanthocephalus* (pronounced *zan-tho-SEFF-ah-lus*), so X is for blackbird. Can you think of any other bird or animal names starting with X? This colorful resident of freshwater marshes and sloughs builds its nest, a woven cup fastened to reeds, tules, or willows, in colonies with other birds.

This natural boulder arch is located in Big Bend's Grapevine Hills at the end of a 2.2-mile trail.

BIG BEND NATIONAL PARK is located in Texas on its boundary with Mexico along the Rio Grande. The park is important because it protects over 800,000 acres, including the Chisos Mountains, vast expanses of desert, and the habitat along 118 miles of the Rio Grande. The park is named for the sharp bend in the river where its southeasterly flow turns abruptly to the northeast. Big Bend preserves the largest area of Chihuahuan Desert in the United States.

The song of the male yellow-headed blackbird is a grating series of high-pitched rasping and rattling notes that has been compared to the sound of a rusty hinge.

BIG BEND NATIONAL PARK

Y IS FOR YELLOWLEGS

The greater yellowlegs is a common shorebird about a foot in length. When an intruder approaches, this wader quickly takes flight. As it flies, its long legs extend out beyond its whitish rump and tail. The bird's call is a frequently-repeated cry of 3 to 5 notes that are clear, loud, and whistle-like. While walking, the yellowlegs bobs its body in an up-and-down motion.

Limantour Spit is a long, thin finger of land bound between Drakes Bay and an estuary. Scores of shorebirds feed in the wetlands and along the sandy spit during the fall.

POINT REYES NATIONAL SEASHORE is located on the coast of the Pacific Ocean just north of San Francisco in northern California. The seashore is important because it protects a stunning natural landscape of thundering ocean breakers, open grasslands, brushy hillsides, and forested ridges. This coastal sanctuary provides a home for nearly 20% of the plants that occur in California and 45% of the bird species that have been recorded in the United States.

Rather than probe the sand and ground with its bill, the yellowlegs uses it to skim the water's surface or swings it through shallow water or pools in search of food.

POINT REYES NATIONAL SEASHORE

Z IS FOR ZOOLOGIST

Many women and men work to protect and care for the animals that live in the national parks. A person trained to do this job is called a zoologist (pronounced *zo-all-uh-jist*) or wildlife biologist. These scientists make sure that park animals stay healthy and that the places where they live are not damaged or destroyed.

The National Park Service manages animals and plants and their environments to minimize any harmful effects of people using the parks.

THE NATIONAL PARK SERVICE was established in 1916 to care for and manage the national parks and monuments of the United States. One of its jobs is to protect the parklands so that birds, reptiles, amphibians, and mammals can live safely. The park service includes researchers, scientists, resource managers, and wildlife biologists, and they all work to learn everything they can so that animals are safeguarded for future generations of Americans.

If conditions are proper, the National Park Service restores animal species in parks from which they were eliminated by humans.

THE NATIONAL PARK SERVICE

NATIONAL PARKS, MONUMENTS, AND SEASHORES INCLUDED IN THIS BOOK

OLYMPIC NP

GLACIER NP

THEODORE
ROOSEVELT NP

ACADIA NP

CRATER LAKE NP

YELLOWSTONE NP

GRAND TETON NP

POINT REYES NS

ROCKY MOUNTAIN NP

YOSEMITE NP

ZION NP

CANYONLANDS NP

SEQUOIA/KINGS
CANYON NP

BRYCE CANYON NP

DEATH VALLEY NP

GRAND CANYON NP

PETRIFIED FOREST NP

GREAT SMOKY MOUNTAINS NP

SAGUARO NP

CHIRICAHUA NM

BIG BEND NP

EVERGLADES NP

DENALI NP

HAWAI'I VOLCANOES NP

THE NATIONAL PARK SERVICE
  1849 C Street NW
  Washington, DC 20240
  Phone: (202) 208-6843
  Web site: http://www.nps.gov
  The Learning Place: http://www.nps.gov/interp/learn.htm
  Wildlife and Plants: http://www1.nature.nps.gov/wv/

ACADIA NATIONAL PARK
  P.O. Box 177
  Bar Harbor, ME 04609-0177
  Phone: (207) 288-3338 (Voice and TDD)
  Email: Acadia_Information@nps.gov
  Web site: http://www.nps.gov/acad/

BIG BEND NATIONAL PARK
  P.O. Box 129
  Big Bend National Park, TX 79834
  Phone: (915) 477-2251
  Email: BIBE_Information@nps.gov
  Web site: http://www.nps.gov/bibe/

BRYCE CANYON NATIONAL PARK
  P.O. Box 170001
  Bryce Canyon, UT 84717-0001
  Phone: (435) 834-5322
  Email: BRCA_Superintendent@nps.gov
  Web site: http://www.nps.gov/brca/

CANYONLANDS NATIONAL PARK
  2282 S. West Resource Blvd.
  Moab, UT 84532-3298
  Phone: (435) 719-2313
  Email: canyinfo@nps.gov
  Web site: http://www.nps.gov/cany/

CHIRICAHUA NATIONAL MONUMENT
  HCR 2, Box 6500
  Willcox, AZ 85643-9737
  Phone: (520) 824-3560
  Email: CHIR_Superintendent@nps.gov
  Web site: http://www.nps.gov/chir/

CRATER LAKE NATIONAL PARK
  P.O. Box 7
  Crater Lake, OR 97604
  Phone: (541) 594-2211
  Email: Craterlake_Info@nps.gov
  Web site: http://www.nps.gov/crla/

DEATH VALLEY NATIONAL PARK
  P.O. Box 579
  Death Valley, CA 92328
  Phone: (760) 786-2331
  Email: DEVA_Superintendent@nps.gov
  Web site: http://www.nps.gov/deva/

DENALI NATIONAL PARK
  Superintendent's Office
  P.O. Box 9
  Denali Park, AK 99755
  Phone: (907) 683-2294
  Email: denali_info@nps.gov
  Web site: http://www.nps.gov/dena/

EVERGLADES NATIONAL PARK
40001 State Road 9336
Homestead, FL 33034-6733
Phone: (305) 242-7700
Email: EVER_Information@nps.gov
Web site: http://www.nps.gov/ever/

GLACIER NATIONAL PARK
Park Headquarters
West Glacier, MT 59936
Phone: (406) 888-7800
Email: glac_park_info@nps.gov
Web site: http://www.nps.gov/glac/

GRAND CANYON NATIONAL PARK
P.O. Box 129
Grand Canyon, AZ 86023
Phone: (520) 638- 7888
Email: GRCA_Superintendent@nps.gov
Web site: http://www.nps.gov/grca/

GRAND TETON NATIONAL PARK
P.O. Drawer 170
Moose, WY 83012-0170
Phone: (307) 739-3300
Email: GRTE_Info@nps.gov
Web site: http://www.nps.gov/grte/

GREAT SMOKY MOUNTAINS NATIONAL PARK
107 Park Headquarters Road
Gatlinburg, TN 37738
Phone: (865) 436-1200
Email: grsm_smokies_information@nps.gov
Web site: http://www.nps.gov/grsm/

HAWAI'I VOLCANOES NATIONAL PARK
P.O. Box 52
Hawai'i National Park, HI 96718-0052
Phone: (808) 985-6000
Email: Norrie_Judd@nps.gov
Web site: http://www.nps.gov/havo/

Kings Canyon National Park – see Sequoia and Kings Canyon National Parks

OLYMPIC NATIONAL PARK
600 East Park Avenue
Port Angeles, WA 98362-6798
Phone: (360) 452-0330
Email: olym_olympic_park_vc@nps.gov
Web site: http://www.nps.gov/olym/

PETRIFIED FOREST NATIONAL PARK
P.O. Box 2217
Petrified Forest National Park, AZ 86028
Phone: (520) 524-6228
Email: PEFO_Superintendent@nps.gov
Web site: http://www.nps.gov/pefo/

POINT REYES NATIONAL SEASHORE
Point Reyes, CA 94956
Phone: (415) 464-5100
Email: PORE_Webmaster@nps.gov
Web site: http://www.nps.gov/pore/

ROCKY MOUNTAIN NATIONAL PARK
1000 Highway 36
Estes Park, CO 80517-8397
Phone: (970) 586-1206
Email: ROMO_Information@nps.gov
Web site: http://www.nps.gov/romo/

SAGUARO NATIONAL PARK
  3693 South Old Spanish Trail
  Tucson, AZ 85730-5601
  Phone: (520) 733-5153
  Email: SAGU_Information@nps.gov
  Web site: http://www.nps.gov/sagu/

SEQUOIA AND KINGS CANYON NATIONAL PARKS
  47050 Generals Highway
  Three Rivers, CA 93271-9651
  Phone: (559) 565-3341
  Email: SEKI_Superintendent@nps.gov
  Web site: http://www.nps.gov/seki/

THEODORE ROOSEVELT NATIONAL PARK
  P.O. Box 7
  Medora, ND 58645-0007
  Phone: (701) 623-4466
  Email: susan_reece@nps.gov
  Web site: http://www.nps.gov/thro/

YELLOWSTONE NATIONAL PARK
  P.O. Box 168
  Yellowstone National Park, WY 82190
  Phone: (307) 344-7381
  Email: yell_visitor_services@nps.gov
  Web site: http://www.nps.gov/yell/

YOSEMITE NATIONAL PARK
  PO Box 577
  Yosemite National Park, CA 95389
  Phone: (209) 372-0200
  Email: yose_web_manager@nps.gov
  Web site: http://www.nps.gov/yose/

ZION NATIONAL PARK
  SR9
  Springdale, UT 84767-1099
  Phone: (435) 772-3256
  Email: ZION_park_information@nps.gov
  Web site: http://www.nps.gov/zion/

NATIONAL PARK AND WILDLIFE RESOURCES

CORNELL LAB OF ORNITHOLOGY
  The lab is devoted to the study and protection of birds.
  Its web site has a wealth of information including an online
  field guide, a bird source map, and bird facts and FAQs.

  P.O. Box 11
  Ithaca, NY 14851
  Phone: (800) 843-2473
  Web site: http://birds.cornell.edu

DEFENDERS OF WILDLIFE
  An organization dedicated to the protection of all native
  wild animals and plants in their natural communities.

  1101 14th Street, N.W. #1400
  Washington, DC 20005
  Phone: (202) 682-9400
  Web site: http://www.defenders.org
  Kid's Planet: http://www.kidsplanet.org/

HAWAI'I WILDLIFE FUND
  An organization dedicated to the preservation of Hawaii's native
  wildlife through research, education, and conservation.

  P.O. Box 637
  Paia, Maui, HI 96779
  Web site: http://www.wildhawaii.org

INTERNATIONAL WOLF CENTER

An organization that supports the survival of the wolf around the world by teaching about its life, its association with other species, and its relationship to humans.

1396 Highway 169
Ely, MN 55731-8129
Phone: (218) 365-4695
Web site: http://www.wolf.org

MOUNTAIN LION FOUNDATION

A conservation and education organization dedicated to protecting the mountain lion, its wild habitat, and the wildlife that shares that habitat.

P.O. Box 1896
Sacramento, CA 95812
Phone: (916) 442-2666
Web site: http://www.mountainlion.org
Just for Kids: http://www.mountainlion.org/Kids/kids.htm

NATIONAL AUDUBON SOCIETY

An organization working to conserve and restore natural ecosystems, focusing on birds and other wildlife, for the benefit of humanity and the earth's biological diversity.

700 Broadway
New York, NY 10003
Phone: (212) 979-3000
Web site: http://www.audubon.org
Audubon Education: http://www.audubon.org/educate/

NATIONAL BIGHORN SHEEP CENTER

An organization dedicated to educating the public about the habitat and conservation needs of the Rocky Mountain Bighorn Sheep.

P.O. Box 1435
Dubois, WY 82513
Phone: (307) 455-3429
Web site: http://www.bighorn.org
Traveling Trunks: http://www.bighorn.org/exhibit.html

NATIONAL PARK FOUNDATION

An organization that encourages private donations for the benefit of the national park system, and for the conservation of its natural, scenic, historic, scientific, and educational resources.

1101 17th Street, N.W., Suite 1102
Washington, DC 20036-4704
Phone: (202) 785-4500
Web site: http://www.nationalparks.org

NATIONAL PARKS CONSERVATION ASSOCIATION

An organization dedicated to protecting the national park system and its natural, historic, and cultural heritage for the next generation.

1300 19th Streeet, N.W., Suite 300
Washington, DC 20036
Phone: (800) 628-7275
Web site: http://www.npca.org
Protecting Wildlife: http://www.npca.org/wildlife_protection/

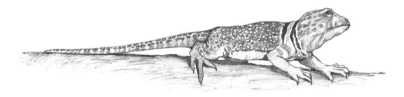

NATIONAL WILDLIFE FEDERATION

An organization working to educate, inspire, and assist individuals and organizations to conserve wildlife and other natural resources and to protect the Earth's environment.

11100 Wildlife Center Drive
Reston, VA 20190-5362
Phone: (703) 438-6000
Web site: http://www.nwf.org
Ranger Rick's Kids Zone: http://www.nwf.org/nwf/kids/

NORTH AMERICAN BEAR CENTER

An organization working to provide understanding and appreciation of black bears, their role in the ecosystem, and their relationship to humans.

P. O. Box 161
Ely, MN 55731
Web site: http://www.bear.org
Just for Kids: http://www.bear.org/Just-For-Kids/index.htm

THE PEREGRINE FUND

An organization that focuses on birds to conserve nature by restoring species in jeopardy, conserving habitat, educating students, and training conservationists.

566 West Flying Hawk Lane
Boise, ID 83709
Phone: (208) 362-3716
Web site: http://www.peregrinefund.org

PETERSON ONLINE BIRDS

This web site is a fine way to learn about bird identification using such features as Peterson's Perspectives, Identifications, and the Skill Builder. There are thorough accounts for many birds.

Web site: http://www.petersononline.com

U.S. FISH AND WILDLIFE SERVICE

An agency of the U.S. government that helps protect a healthy environment for people, fish, and wildlife, and that helps Americans conserve fish, wildlife, and plants.

1849 C Street, N.W.
Washington DC 20240
Phone: (202) 208-4131
Web site: http://www.fws.gov
Especially for Kids: http://www.fws.gov/kids/

U.S. GEOLOGICAL SURVEY PATUXENT WILDLIFE RESEARCH CENTER

A U.S. government research institute for wildlife and natural resource science, providing information to better manage the nation's biological resources.

12100 Beech Forest Road, Suite 4039
Laurel, MD 20708-4039
Phone: (301) 497-5500
Web site: http://www.pwrc.usgs.gov

THE WILDERNESS SOCIETY

An organization that works to protect America's wilderness and to develop a nation-wide network of wild lands through public education, scientific analysis, and advocacy.

1615 M St, N.W.
Washington, DC 20036
Phone: (800) THE-WILD
Web site: http://www.wildernesssociety.org
Kids Corner: http://www.wilderness.org/kidscorner/index.htm

WORLD WILDLIFE FUND

An organization dedicated to protecting the world's wildlife and wildlands.

1250 24th Street, N.W.
P.O. Box 97180
Washington, DC 20037
Phone: (800) CALL-WWF
Web site: http://www.worldwildlife.org
Kid's Stuff: http://www.worldwildlife.org/fun/kids.cfm

ACKNOWLEDGEMENTS

Thanks to the following fine people who reviewed spreads,
answered questions, and served as subject experts during
the preparation of this book.

Kevin Bacher, Crater Lake NP
Karen A. Beppler, Petrified Forest NP
Sarah Bourbon, Big Bend NP
Curt Buchholtz, Rocky Mountain NP
Ginger Burley, Yosemite NP
Pat Cole, Yellowstone NP
Tom Danton, Saguaro NP
Kathy English, Hawai'i NHA
Marty Feldner, Arizona Herpetological Society
Mark Flippo, Big Bend NP
Pam Frazier, Grand Canyon NP
Larry Frederick, Glacier NP
Beryl Given, Everglades NP
John Gunn, Rocky Mountain NP
Lyman Hafen, Zion NP
Paul Henderson, Canyonlands NP
Paula Henrie, Bryce Canyon NP
Wendy Hill, Glacier NP
Darcy Hu, Hawai'i Volcanoes NP
Bruce M. Kaye, Theodore Roosevelt NP
Steve Kemp, Great Smoky Mountains NP
Jan Lynch, Grand Teton NP
Jeff Maugans, Rocky Mountain NP
Len McKenzie, Point Reyes NS
Charley Money, Alaska NHA
Suzanne Moody, Chiricahua NM
Wanda Moran, Acadia NP
Jane Muggli, Theodore Roosevelt NP
Janice Newton, Death Valley NP
Laurie Pohll, Crater Lake NP
Jack Potter, Glacier NP
Roger Rudolph, Olympic NP
Tessy Shirakawa, Petrified Forest NP
LeAnn Simpson, Glacier NHA
Steve Thompson, Yosemite NP
Mark Tilchen, Sequoia NHA
Brad Wallis, Canyonlands NHA